HORRID HENRY

TERRIBLE TEACHERS

FRANCESCA SIMON

FRANCESCA SIMON SPENT HER CHILDHOOD ON THE BEACH IN CALIFORNIA AND STARTED WRITING STORIES AT THE AGE OF EIGHT. SHE WROTE HER FIRST HORRID HENRY BOOK IN 1994. HORRID HENRY HAS GONE ON TO CONQUER THE GLOBE; HIS ADVENTURES HAVE SOLD MILLIONS OF COPIES WORLDWIDE.

FRANCESCA HAS WON THE CHILDREN'S BOOK OF THE YEAR AWARD AND IN 2009 WAS AWARDED A GOLD BLUE PETER BADGE. SHE WAS ALSO A TRUSTEE OF THE WORLD BOOK DAY CHARITY FOR SIX YEARS.

FRANCESCA LIVES IN NORTH LONDON WITH HER FAMILY.

WWW.FRANCESCASIMON.COM WWW.HORRIDHENRY.CO.UK @SIMON_FRANCESCA

TONY ROSS

TONY ROSS WAS BORN IN LONDON AND STUDIED AT THE LIVERPOOL SCHOOL OF ART AND DESIGN. HE HAS WORKED AS A CARTOONIST, A GRAPHIC DESIGNER, AN ADVERTISING ART DIRECTOR AND A UNIVERSITY LECTURER.

TONY IS ONE OF THE MOST POPULAR AND SUCCESSFUL CHILDREN'S ILLUSTRATORS OF ALL TIME, BEST KNOWN FOR ILLUSTRATING HORRID HENRY AND THE WORKS OF DAVID WALLIAMS, AS WELL AS HIS OWN HUGELY POPULAR SERIES, THE LITTLE PRINCESS. HE LIVES IN MACCLESFIELD.

HORRID HENRY

TERRIBLE TEACHERS

FRANCESCA SIMON

ILLUSTRATED BY TONY ROSS

Orion

ORION CHILDREN'S BOOKS

Stories originally published in "Horrid Henry", "Horrid Henry's Nits", "Horrid Henry Gets Rich Quick", "Horrid Henry's Revenge", "Horrid Henry's Stinkbombs" and "Horrid Henry Wakes the Dead" respectively.

This collection first published in Great Britain in 2023 by Hodder and Stoughton

3 5 7 9 10 8 6 4 2

A CIP catalogue record for this book is available from the British Library.

ISBN 978 1 5101 1132 5

Printed and bound in Great Britain by Clays Ltd, Elcograf S.P.A.

The paper and board used in this book are from well-managed forests and other responsible sources.

MIX
Paper from
responsible sources
FSC
www.fsc.org   FSC® C104740

Orion Children's Books
An imprint of
Hachette Children's Group
Part of Hodder and Stoughton Limited
Carmelite House
50 Victoria Embankment
London EC4Y 0DZ

An Hachette UK Company
www.hachette.co.uk

www.hachettechildrens.co.uk
www.horridhenry.co.uk

CONTENTS

MEET THE

200 CM

175 CM

150 CM   HENRY   PETER

125 CM

100 CM

75 CM

50 CM

25 CM

0 CM

GANG

MUM AND DAD

MARGARET

RALPH

HORRID HENRY'S

DANCE CLASS

STOMP STOMP STOMP STOMP STOMP STOMP STOMP.

Horrid Henry was practising his elephant dance.

Tap Tap Tap Tap Tap Tap Tap Tap.

Perfect Peter was practising his raindrop dance.

Peter was practising being a raindrop for his dance class show.

Henry was also supposed to be practising being a raindrop.

But Henry did not want to be a raindrop. He did not want to be a **tomato**, a **string bean** or a banana either.

STOMP STOMP STOMP

went Henry's heavy boots.

Tap Tap Tap went Peter's tap shoes.

"You're doing it wrong, Henry," said Peter.

"No I'm not," said Henry.

"You are too," said Peter. "We're supposed to be raindrops."

STOMP STOMP STOMP went Henry's boots. He was an elephant smashing his way through the jungle, trampling on everyone who stood in his way.

"I can't concentrate with you stomping," said Peter. "And I have to practise my solo."

"WHO CARES?" screamed Horrid Henry. "I HATE DANCING, I HATE DANCE CLASS, AND MOST OF ALL, I HATE YOU!"

This was not entirely true. Horrid Henry loved dancing. Henry danced in his bedroom. Henry danced up and down the stairs. Henry danced on the new sofa and on the kitchen table.

What Henry *HATED* was having
to dance with other children.

"Couldn't I go to **karate** instead?"
asked Henry every Saturday.

"No," said Mum.
"Too violent."

"Judo?" said Henry.

"N-O SPELLS NO," said Dad.

14

So every Saturday morning
at 9.45 a.m., Henry and
Peter's father drove
them to Miss Impatience
Tutu's Dance Studio.

Miss Impatience Tutu
was skinny and bony. She
had long stringy grey
hair. Her nose was SHARP.
Her elbows were POINTY. Her
knees were knobbly.
No one had ever seen
her smile.

Perhaps this was because

Impatience Tutu hated teaching.

Impatience Tutu hated noise.

Impatience Tutu hated children.

But most of all Impatience Tutu hated **Horrid Henry**.

This was not surprising. When Miss Tutu shouted, "**CLASS, LIFT YOUR LEFT LEGS**," eleven left legs lifted. One right leg sagged to the floor.

When Miss Tutu screamed, "**HEEL, TOE, HEEL, TOE**," eleven dainty feet tapped away. One clumpy foot stomped toe, heel, toe, heel.

When Miss Tutu bellowed, "**CLASS,**

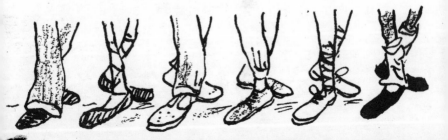

SKIP TO YOUR RIGHT," eleven bodies turned to the right. One body galumphed to the left.

Naturally, no one wanted to dance with Henry. Or indeed, anywhere near Henry. Today's class, unfortunately, was no different.

"Miss Tutu, Henry is treading on my toes," said Jumpy Jeffrey.

"Miss Tutu, Henry is kicking my legs," said Lazy Linda.

"Miss Tutu, Henry is bumping me," said Vain Violet.

"**HENRY!**" screeched Miss Tutu.

"Yeah," said Henry.

"I am a *patient* woman, and you are trying my patience to the limit," hissed Miss Tutu. "Any more bad behaviour and you will be very sorry."

"What will happen?" asked Horrid Henry eagerly.

Miss Tutu stood very tall. She took a LONG, BONY FINGER and dragged it slowly across her throat.

Henry decided that he would rather live to do battle another day. He stood on the side, gnashing his teeth, pretending he was an ENORMOUS

crocodile about to gobble up Miss Tutu.

"This is our final rehearsal before the show," **BARKED** Miss Tutu. "Everything must be perfect."

Eleven faces stared at Miss Tutu. One face scowled at the floor.

"Tomatoes and beans to the front," ordered Miss Tutu. "When Miss Thumper plays the music everyone will *STRETCH* out their arms to the sky, to *kiss* the morning hello. Raindrops, stand at the back next to the giant green leaves and wait until the beans find the magic bananas.

"And Henry," spat Miss Tutu, glaring. "TRY TO GET IT RIGHT."

"Positions, everybody. Miss Thumper, the opening music please!" shouted Miss Tutu.

Miss Thumper banged away.

The tomatoes weaved in and out, twirling.

The beans
pirouetted.

The
bananas
pointed
their toes
and *swayed.*

The raindrops *pitter-patted.*

All except one. Henry waved his
arms *FRANTICALLY* and raced
round the room. Then he

crashed into the beans.

"**HENRY!**" screeched Miss Tutu.

"Yeah," scowled Henry.

"Sit in the corner!"

Henry was delighted. He sat in the corner and made horrible rude faces while Peter did his raindrop solo.

TAP TAP TAP TAP TAP TAP TAP. TAPPA TAPPA TAPPA TAPPA TAP TAP TAP. TAPPA TIP TAPPA TIP TAPPA TAPPA TAPPA TIP.

"Was that perfect, Miss Tutu?" asked Peter.

Miss Tutu sighed. "Perfect, Peter, as always," she said, and the corner of her mouth trembled slightly.

This was the closest Miss Tutu

ever came to smiling.

Then she saw Henry slouching on the chair. Her mouth drooped back into its normal grim position.

Miss Tutu *tugged* Henry off the chair. She **SHOVED** him to the very back of the stage, behind the other raindrops. Then she **pushed** him behind a giant green leaf.

"**STAND THERE!**" shouted Miss Tutu.

"But no one will see me here," said Henry.

"Precisely," said Miss Tutu.

It was showtime.

The curtain was about to rise.

The children stood quietly on
stage.

Perfect Peter was so excited he
almost BOUNCED up and down.
Naturally he controlled himself and
stood still.

Horrid Henry was not very excited.
He did not want to be a raindrop.
And he certainly did not want to be a

raindrop who danced behind a giant
green leaf.

Miss Thumper *waddled* over to the
piano. She **banged** on the keys.

The curtain went up.

Henry's mum and dad were in the audience with the other parents. As usual they sat in the back row, in case they had to make a quick getaway.

They smiled and waved at Peter, standing proudly at the front.

"Can you see Henry?" whispered Henry's mum.

Henry's dad squinted at the stage.

A tuft of red hair stuck up behind
the green leaf.

"*I think that's him behind the leaf,*"
said his father doubtfully.

"*I wonder why Henry is hiding,*"
said Mum. "*It's not like him to be shy.*"

"Hmmmm," said Dad.

"SHHH," hissed the parents beside them.

Henry watched the tomatoes and beans searching on tiptoe for the magic bananas.

I'm not staying back here, he thought, and pushed his way through the raindrops.

"Stop pushing, Henry!" hissed Lazy Linda.

Henry pushed **HARDER**,
then did a few pitter-pats with the other
raindrops.

Miss Tutu stretched out a *bony*
arm and *yanked* Henry back behind
the scenery.

Who wants to be a raindrop
anyway, thought Henry. I can do
what I like hidden here.

The tomatoes weaved in and out,
twirling.

The beans pirouetted.

The bananas pointed their toes
and *swayed*.

The raindrops pitter-patted. Henry flapped his arms and pretended he was a pterodactyl about to pounce on Miss Tutu.

Round and round he flew, homing in on his prey.

Perfect Peter stepped to the front and began his solo.

TAP TAP TAP
TAP TAP TAP
TAP TAP TAP
TAP TAP TAP

CRASH!

One giant green leaf fell on top of the raindrops, **KNOCKING** them over.

The raindrops **COLLIDED** with the tomatoes.

The tomatoes **SMASHED** into the string beans.

The string beans **BUMPED** into the bananas.

Perfect Peter turned his head to see what was happening and danced off the stage into the front row.

Miss Tutu fainted.

The only person still standing on stage was Henry.

STOMP STOMP STOMP STOMP STOMP STOMP STOMP.

Henry did his elephant dance.

Boom Boom Boom Boom Boom Boom Boom.

Henry did his wild buffalo dance.

Peter tried to scramble back on stage.

The curtain fell.

There was a long silence, then Henry's parents clapped.

No one else did, so Henry's parents stopped.

All the other parents ran up to Miss Tutu and started shouting.

"I don't see why that **HORRID** boy should have had such a long solo while all Linda did was lie on the floor," **yelled** one mother.

"My Jeffrey is a much better dancer than that boy," **SHOUTED** another.

"He should have done the solo."

"I didn't know you taught modern dance, Miss Tutu," said Violet's mother. "Come, Violet," she added, sweeping from the room.

"**HENRY!!**" screeched Miss Tutu. "Leave my dance studio at once!"

"Whoopee!" shouted Henry. He knew that next Saturday he would be at karate class at last.

HORRID HENRY'S
SCHOOL TRIP

"DON'T FORGET MY PACKED LUNCH FOR THE SCHOOL TRIP," shouted Horrid Henry for the tenth time. "I want **CRISPS**, **BISCUITS**, *chocolate* and a **FIZZYWIZZ** drink."

"No way, Henry," said Dad grimly, slicing carrots. "I'm making you a healthy, nutritious lunch."

"But I don't want a healthy lunch," howled Henry. "I like sweets!"

"Sweets, **YUCK**," said Perfect Peter.

He peeked in his lunch box.

"Oh boy, an apple!" said Peter. "And

egg and cress on brown bread with the crusts on! And carrot and celery sticks, my favourite! Thank you so much, Dad. Henry, if you don't eat healthy food, you'll never grow big and strong."

"Oh yeah," said Henry. "I'll show you how **BIG** and **STRONG** I am, you little PIPSQUEAK," he added, springing at Peter. He was a boa constrictor throttling his prey.

"**UGGGHHHH**," choked Peter.

"Stop being *HORRID*, Henry!" shouted Mum. "Or there will be

no school trip for you."

Henry let Peter go. **Horrid Henry** loved school trips. No work. No assembly. A packed lunch. A chance to fool around all day. What could be better?

"I'm going to the FROSTY FREEZE ICE CREAM factory," said Henry. "Free ice creams for everyone. **Yippee!**"

Perfect Peter made a face. "I don't like ice cream," he said. "My class is going somewhere much better — our Town Museum. And Mum's coming to help."

"I'd rather be boiled alive and eaten by **CANNIBALS** than go to that boring old dump," said Horrid Henry, shuddering. Mum had *dragged* him there once. Never again.

Then Henry noticed Peter's T-shirt. It was exactly the same as his, purple striped with gold stars.

"Tell Peter to stop copying what I wear to school!" **SCREAMED** Henry.

"It doesn't matter, Henry," said Mum. "You're going on different trips. No one will notice."

"Just keep out of my way, Peter,"

snarled Henry. "I don't want anyone to think we're related."

Horrid Henry's class **buzzed** with excitement as they scrambled to be first on the bus.

"I've got **CRISPS!**" shouted Dizzy Dave.

"I've got **BISCUITS!**" shouted Anxious Andrew.

"I've got **toffee** and *chocolate* and LOLLIES and three **FIZZY WIZZES!**" shouted Greedy Graham.

"**WAAAA**," wailed Weepy William. "I forgot my packed lunch."

"**QUIET!**" ordered Miss Battle-Axe as the bus started moving. "Sit still and behave. **NO EATING** on the bus. William, stop weeping."

"**I need a wee!**" shouted Lazy Linda.

"Well, you'll have to wait," snapped Miss Battle-Axe.

Horrid Henry had **trampled** his way to the window seats at the back next to Rude Ralph and Greedy Graham. He liked those seats best.

Miss Battle-Axe couldn't see him, and he could make faces at all the people in the cars behind him.

Henry and Ralph rolled down the window and chanted:

"BEANS, BEANS, GOOD FOR THE HEART, THE MORE YOU EAT, THE MORE YOU–"

"**HENRY!**" bellowed Miss Battle-Axe. "Turn around and face forward **NOW!**"

"**I need a wee!**" shouted Dizzy Dave.

"Look what I've got, Henry," said Greedy Graham, holding a bulging bag of sweets.

"Gimme some," said Henry.

"And me," said Rude Ralph.

The three boys stuffed their faces with sweets.

"**UGH**, a green lime," said Henry, taking the sticky sweet out of his mouth. "**EEECH**." He flicked the sweet away.

PING!

The sweet landed on Moody
Margaret's neck.

"**OW**," said Margaret.

She turned round and glared
at Henry.

"Stop it, Henry!" she snarled.

"I didn't do anything," said
Henry.

PING!

A sweet landed in Sour Susan's
hair.

PING!

A sweet stuck on Anxious
Andrew's new jumper.

"Henry's throwing sweets!" shouted Margaret.

Miss Battle-Axe turned round.

"Henry! Sit next to me," she said.

"I need a wee!" wailed Weepy William.

Finally, the bus drove up to the
FROSTY FREEZE factory.

A gigantic, delicious-looking ice cream
cone loomed above it.

"We're here!" shouted Henry.

"YOU SCREAM! I SCREAM! WE
ALL SCREAM FOR ICE CREAM!"
shrieked the children as the bus
stopped outside the gate.

"Why are we waiting here?" yelled
Greedy Graham. "I want my ice
creams **NOW!**"

Henry stuck his head out of the
window. The gates were chained shut.

A large sign read:

CLOSED ON MONDAYS.

Miss Battle-Axe looked pale. "I don't believe this," she muttered.

"Class, there's been a mix-up, and we seem to have come on the wrong day," said Miss Battle-Axe. "But never mind. We'll go to—"

"The Science Museum!" shouted Clever Clare.

"The zoo!" shouted Dizzy Dave.

"Laser Zap!" shouted Horrid Henry.

"No," said Miss Battle-Axe. "Our Town Museum."

"UGGGGHHHHH," groaned the class.

No one groaned louder than Horrid Henry.

The children left their jackets and lunch boxes in the packed lunch room, and then followed the museum guide to Room 1.

"First we'll see Mr Jones's collection of *rubber bands*," said the guide. "Then our famous display of *door hinges* and *dog collars* through history. And don't worry, you'll be seeing our latest acquisitions, **soil** from Miss Montague's garden and the Mayor's **baby** pictures."

Horrid Henry had to escape.

"**I need a wee**," said Henry.

"Hurry up then," said Miss Battle-Axe. "And come straight back."

The toilets were next to the packed lunch room.

Henry thought he'd make sure his lunch was still there. Yup, there it was, right next to Ralph's.

I wonder what Ralph has got,

thought Henry, staring at Ralph's
packed lunch. No harm in looking.

WOW. Rude Ralph's lunch box was
bursting with **CRISPS**, *sweets* and a
chocolate spread sandwich on white
bread.

He'll feel **SICK** if he eats all that
junk food, thought Henry. I'd better
help him.

It was the work of a moment
to swap Ralph's
sandwich for
Henry's egg and
cress.

This certainly isn't very healthy,
thought Henry, gazing at Greedy
Graham's goodies. I'll do him a
favour and exchange a few of my
celery sticks for his sweets.

Just look at all those treats,
thought Henry, fingering Sour
Susan's cakes. She should eat a more
balanced meal.

A pack of raisins zipped from Henry's lunch box to Susan's and a *sticky bun* leapt from Susan's to Henry's.

Tsk tsk, thought Henry, helping himself to Tough Toby's chocolate bar and replacing it with an apple. Too many *sweets* are bad for the teeth.

That's better, he thought, gazing at his re-packed lunch with satisfaction. Then he *strolled* back to his class, who were gathered round a glass case.

"This is the **soil** in which Miss Montague grew her prize-winning vegetables," droned the guide. "She grew marrows, tomatoes, potatoes, leeks—"

"WHEN DO WE EAT?" interrupted Horrid Henry.

"I'm starving," whined Greedy Graham.

"My tummy's **RUMBLING**," groaned Rude Ralph.

"When's lunch?" moaned Moody Margaret.

"WE'RE HUNGRY!"

wailed the children.

"All right," said Miss Battle-Axe. "We'll eat now."

The class **stampeded** down the hall and *grabbed* their lunches. Henry sat in a corner and tucked in.

For a moment there was silence, then the room echoed with howls of dismay.

"Where's my sticky bun?" yelped Sour Susan.

"My sweets are gone!" screamed Greedy Graham.

"What's this? Egg and cress? YUCK!" shouted Rude Ralph, hurling the sandwich at Anxious Andrew.

That did it. The room filled with flying carrot and celery sticks,

granola bars, raisins, crusts and
apples. Henry smirked as he wiped
the last traces of chocolate from his
mouth.

"STOP IT! STOP IT!"

howled Miss Battle-Axe.

"Well done, Henry, for being the only sensible child. You may lead us back to see the pieces of Roman pottery in Room 2."

Horrid Henry walked proudly at the head of the shuffling, WHINING children. Then he noticed the lift at the far end. A sign read:

STAFF ONLY: DO NOT ENTER

I wonder where that lift goes, thought Horrid Henry.

"**STOP HIM!**" yelled a guard.

But it was too late.

Henry had *dashed* to the lift and pressed the top button.

Up up up he zipped.

Henry found himself in a small room filled with half-finished exhibits. On display were lists of overdue library books, "Lightbulbs from 1965 to today," and rows and rows of rocks.

Then, in the corner, Henry actually

saw something interesting: a
dog's SKELETON protected by a
drooping blue cord.

Henry looked more closely.

It's just a pile of bones, thought
Henry.

He wobbled the blue cord then
stood on it.

"Look at me, I'm a tight-rope walker," **CHORTLED** Horrid Henry, swaying on the blue cord. "I'm the best tight-rope walker in—

AGGGHHHH!"

Horrid Henry lost his balance and toppled against the skeleton.

CLITTER-CLATTER!

The bones crashed to the ground.
DING DING DING. A burglar
alarm began to wail.

Museum guards ran into the room.

Uh-oh, thought Horrid Henry.
He *slipped* between a guard's legs
and **ran**. Behind him he could hear
pounding feet.

Henry *dashed* into a large room
filled with road signs, used bus
tickets and traffic cones. At the other
end of the room Henry saw Peter's
class gathered in front of "The Story
of the Drain". Oh no. There was Mum.

Henry ducked behind the traffic cones.

Museum guards entered.

"**THERE HE IS!**" shouted one. "The boy in the purple T-shirt with the gold stars."

Henry stood *FIXED* to the spot. He was trapped. Then the guards ran straight past his hiding place. A long arm reached over and plucked Perfect Peter from his group.

"Come with us, you!" **snarled** the guard. "We're going straight to the **Bad Children's Room**."

"But . . . but . . ." GASPED Peter.

"No ifs or buts!" snapped the guard. "Who's in charge of this child?"

"I am," said Mum. "What's the meaning of this?"

"You come too," ordered the guard.

"But . . . but . . ." GASPED Mum.

SHOUTING and **PROTESTING**, Mum and Perfect Peter were taken away.

Then Henry heard a familiar **booming** voice.

"Margaret, that's enough pushing," said Miss Battle-Axe. "**No** touching, Ralph. **STOP** weeping, William. Hurry up, everyone! The bus leaves in five minutes. Walk quietly to the exit."

Everyone immediately started running.

Horrid Henry waited until most of the children had charged past then rejoined the group.

"Where have you been, Henry?" *SNAPPED* Miss Battle-Axe.

65

"Just enjoying this brilliant museum," said Horrid Henry. "When can we come back?"

HORRID
HENRY'S
SPORTS DAY

"We all want sports day to be a great success tomorrow," announced Miss Battle-Axe. "I am here to make sure that *no one*" — she glared at Horrid Henry — "SPOILS it."

Horrid Henry glared back. Horrid Henry hated sports day. Last year he hadn't won a single event. He'd dropped his egg in the egg-and-spoon race, TRIPPED over Rude Ralph in the three-legged race, and collided with Sour Susan in the sack race. Henry's team had even lost the tug-of-war.

Most sickening of all, Perfect Peter had won *both* his races.

If only the school had a sensible day, like TV-watching day, or chocolate-eating day, or who could **guzzle** the most crisps day, **Horrid Henry** would be sure to win every prize. But no. *He* had to *leap* and *dash* about getting hot and bothered in front of stupid parents. When he became king he'd make teachers run all the races then behead the winners. **KING HENRY THE HORRIBLE** grinned happily.

"Pay attention, Henry!" barked Miss

70

Battle-Axe. "What did I just say?"

Henry had no idea. "Sports day is cancelled?" he suggested hopefully.

Miss Battle-Axe fixed him with her steely eyes. "I said no one is to bring any sweets tomorrow. You'll all be given a delicious, refreshing piece of orange."

Henry slumped in his chair, SCOWLING. All he could do was hope for rain.

Sports day dawned bright and sunny.

71

RATS, thought Henry. He could, of course, pretend to be sick. But he'd tried that last year and Mum hadn't been **FOOLED**. The year before that he'd complained he'd hurt his leg. Unfortunately Dad then caught him *dancing* on the table.

It was no use. He'd just have to take part. If only he could win a race!

Perfect Peter **BOUNCED** into his room.

"Sports day today!" beamed Peter. "And *I'm* responsible for bringing the hard-boiled **eggs** for the egg-and-spoon races. Isn't it exciting!"

"**NO!**" screeched Henry. "Get out
of here!"

"But I only . . ." began Peter.

Henry *leapt* at him, **roaring**. He was
a cowboy lassoing a runaway steer.

"**EEEAAARGH!**" SQUEALED Peter.

"Stop being *HORRID*, Henry!"
shouted Dad. "Or no pocket
money this week!"

Henry let Peter go.

"It's so unfair," he muttered, picking up his clothes from the floor and putting them on. Why did he never win?

Henry reached under his bed and filled his pockets from the secret sweet tin he kept there. **Horrid Henry** was a **master** at eating sweets in school without being detected. At least he could scoff something good while the others were **STUCK** eating dried-up old orange pieces.

Then he **stomped** downstairs. Perfect Peter was busy packing hard-boiled eggs into a carton.

Horrid Henry sat down
SCOWLING and gobbled his
breakfast.

"Good luck, boys," said Mum. "I'll
be there to cheer for you."

"**Humph,**" growled Henry.

"Thanks, Mum," said Peter.
"I expect I'll **win** my egg-and-spoon
race again but of course it doesn't
matter if I don't. It's how you play
that counts."

"**SHUT UP, PETER!**" snarled
Henry. Egg-and-spoon! Egg-and-spoon!

If Henry heard that **DISGUSTING** phrase once more he would start FROTHING at the mouth.

"Mum! Henry told me to shut up," WAILED Peter, "and he ATTACKED me this morning."

"Stop being **HORRID**, Henry," said Mum. "Peter, come with me and we'll comb your hair. I want you to look your best when you win that trophy again."

Henry's blood boiled. He felt like *snatching* those eggs and *hurling* them against the wall.

Then Henry had a wonderful,
SPECTACULAR idea. It was so
wonderful that . . . Henry heard Mum
coming back down the stairs. There
was no time to lose crowing about
his brilliance.

Horrid Henry *ran* to the fridge,
grabbed another egg carton and
SWAPPED it for the box of hard-
boiled ones on the counter.

"Don't forget your eggs, Peter,"
said Mum. She handed the carton
to Peter, who tucked it safely in his
school bag.

Tee hee, thought Horrid Henry.

Henry's class lined up on the playing fields. **FLASH!** A small figure wearing gleaming white trainers *zipped* by. It was Aerobic Al, the fastest boy in Henry's class.

"Gotta run, gotta run, gotta run,"

he chanted, gliding into place beside
Henry. "I will, of course, win every
event," he announced. "I've been
training all year. My dad's got a special
place all ready for my trophies."

"Who wants to race anyway?"
SNEERED Horrid Henry, sneaking
a **yummy gummy fuzzball** into
his mouth.

"Now, teams for the three-legged
race," BARKED Miss Battle-Axe into
her megaphone. "This is a race showing
how well you co-operate and use
teamwork with your partner. Ralph

will race with William, Josh will race
with Clare, Henry . . ." she glanced
at her list, ". . . you will race with
Margaret."

"**NO!**" screamed Horrid Henry.

"**NO!**" screamed Moody Margaret.

"**YES**," said Miss Battle-Axe.

"But I want to be with Susan," said
Margaret.

"No fussing," said Miss Battle-Axe.
"Bert, where's your partner?"

"I dunno," said Beefy Bert.

Henry and Margaret stood as far
apart as possible while their legs

were tied together.

"You'd better do as I say, Henry," HISSED Margaret. "*I'll* decide how we race."

"*I* will, you mean," HISSED Henry.

"**READY . . . STEADY . . . GO!**"

Miss Battle-Axe blew her whistle.

They were off! Henry moved to the left, Margaret moved to the right.

"**THIS WAY, HENRY!**" shouted Margaret. She tried to drag him.

"**No, this way!**" shouted Henry. He tried to drag her.

They *lurched* wildly, left and right, then **toppled** over.

CRASH! Aerobic Al and Lazy Linda tripped over the *SCREAMING* Henry and Margaret.

SMASH! Rude Ralph and Weepy William fell over Al and Linda.

BUMP! Dizzy Dave and Beefy Bert collided with Ralph and William.

"**WAAA!**" wailed Weepy William.

"It's all your fault, Margaret!" shouted Henry, pulling her hair.

"No, yours," shouted Margaret, pulling his harder.

Miss Battle-Axe blew her whistle frantically.

"**STOP! STOP!**" she ordered. "Henry! Margaret! What an example to set for the younger ones. Any more nonsense like that and you'll be severely punished. Everyone, get ready for the **EGG-AND-SPOON** race!"

This was it! The moment Henry

83

had been waiting for.

The children lined up in their teams. Moody Margaret, Sour Susan and Anxious Andrew were going first in Henry's class. Henry glanced at Peter.

Yes, there he was, smiling proudly, next to Goody-Goody Gordon, Spotless

Sam and Tidy Ted. The eggs lay still on their spoons. Horrid Henry held his breath.

"READY . . . STEADY . . . GO!"

shouted Miss Battle-Axe.

They were off!

"Go, Peter, go!" shouted Mum.

Peter walked *faster* and *faster* and *faster*. He was in the lead. He was pulling away from the field. Then

. . . **wobble . . . wobble . . .**

"AAAAAGH!" yelped Peter.

Moody Margaret's egg wobbled.

Then Susan's.

SPLAT!

Then everybody's.

SPLAT!

SPLAT!

SPLAT!

"I've got egg on my shoes!" wailed Margaret.

"I've ruined my new dress!" SHRIEKED Susan.

"I've got egg all over me!" SQUEALED Tidy Ted.

"Help!" squeaked Perfect Peter. Egg dripped down his trousers.

Parents surged forward, screaming and waving handkerchiefs and towels.

Rude Ralph and Horrid Henry SHRIEKED with laughter.

Miss Battle-Axe blew her whistle.

"Who brought the **eggs?**" asked Miss Battle-Axe. Her voice was like ice.

"I did," said Perfect Peter. "But I brought hard-boiled ones."

"**OUT!**" shouted Miss Battle-Axe.

"Out of the games!"

"But . . . but . . ." gasped Perfect Peter.

"No buts, out!" She glared. "Go straight to the Head."

Perfect Peter **burst** into tears and crept away.

Horrid Henry could hardly contain himself. This was the **BEST** sports day he'd ever been to.

"The rest of you, stop laughing at once. Parents, get back to your seats! Time for the next race!" ordered Miss Battle-Axe.

All things considered, thought **Horrid Henry**, lining up with his class, it hadn't been too *TERRIBLE* a day. He'd loved the egg-and-spoon race, of course. And he'd had **FUN** *pulling* the other team into a muddy puddle in the tug-of-war, knocking over the obstacles in the obstacle race, and **crashing** into Aerobic Al in

the sack race.

But, oh, to actually win something!

There was just one race left before sports day was over. The cross-country run. The event Henry **HATED** more than any other. One long, sweaty, **EXHAUSTING** lap round the whole field.

Henry heaved his heavy bones to the starting line. His final chance to win . . . yet he knew there was no hope. If he beat Weepy William he'd be doing well.

Suddenly Henry had a *wonderful,* **SPECTACULAR IDEA**. Why

90

had he never thought of this before? Truly, he was a genius. Wasn't there some ancient Greek who'd won a race by throwing down golden apples which his rival kept stopping to pick up? Couldn't he, Henry, learn something from those old Greeks?

"READY . . . STEADY . . . GO!" shrieked Miss Battle-Axe.

Off they *dashed*.

"Go, Al, go!" yelled his father.

"Get a move on, Margaret!" **SHRIEKED** her mother.

"Go, Ralph!" cheered his father.

"Do your best, Henry," said Mum.

Horrid Henry reached into his pocket and hurled some sweets. They **THUDDED** to the ground in front of the runners.

"Look, sweets!" shouted Henry.

Al checked behind him. He was well in the lead. He paused and scooped up one sweet, and then another. He glanced behind again, then started unwrapping the **yummy gummy fuzzball**.

"Sweets!" yelped Greedy Graham. He stopped to pick up as many as he

could find then stuffed them in his
mouth.

"*YUMMY!*" screamed Graham.

"*Sweets!* Where?" chanted the
others. Then they stopped to look.

"Over there!" yelled Henry, throwing
another handful. The racers paused
to *pounce* on the treats.

While the others **MUNCHED** and **CRUNCHED**, Henry made a frantic dash for the lead.

He was out in front! Henry's legs moved as they had never moved before, pounding round the field. And there was the finishing line!

THUD! THUD! THUD!

Henry glanced back. Oh no! Aerobic Al was catching up!

Henry felt in his pocket. He had one **GIANT** gob-stopper left. He looked round, panting.

"Go home and take a nap, Henry!"

shouted Al, sticking out his tongue
as he raced past.

Henry threw down the gob-stopper
in front of Al. Aerobic Al hesitated,
then *skidded* to a halt and picked it
up. He could beat Henry any day so
why not show off a bit?

Suddenly Henry *sprinted* past.
Aerobic Al dashed after him. **Harder**
and **harder**, *faster* and *faster* Henry
ran. He was a bird. He was a plane.
He flew across the finishing line.

"The winner is . . . Henry?"
squeaked Miss Battle-Axe.

"I'VE BEEN ROBBED!"
screamed Aerobic Al.

"HURRAY!" yelled Henry.

Wow, what a great day, thought
Horrid Henry, proudly carrying home

his trophy. Al's dad shouting at Miss
Battle-Axe and Mum. Miss Battle-Axe
and Mum shouting back. Peter sent
off in DISGRACE. And he, Henry, the
big winner.

"I can't think how you got those
eggs muddled up," said Mum.

"Me neither," said Perfect Peter,
SNIFFLING.

"Never mind, Peter," said
Henry brightly. "It's not
winning, it's *how you play*
that counts."

HORRID HENRY

AND THE DEMON DINNER LADY

"You're not having a packed lunch and that's final," yelled Dad.

"IT'S NOT FAIR!" yelled Horrid Henry. "Everyone in my class has a packed lunch."

"N-O SPELLS NO," said Dad. "It's too much work. And you **never** eat what I pack for you."

"But I hate school dinners!" screamed Henry. "I'm being POISONED!" He clutched his throat. "Dessert today was – BLECCCCH – fruit salad! And it had **worms** in

it! I can feel them *slithering* in my stomach – **UGGGHH!**" Horrid Henry fell to the floor, **GASPING** and **RASPING**.

Mum continued watching TV.

Dad continued watching TV.

"I love school dinners," said Perfect Peter. "They're so nutritious and delicious. Especially those lovely spinach salads."

"**Shut up, Peter!**" snarled Henry.

"Muuuum!" wailed Peter. "Henry told me to shut up!"

"Don't be **horrid**, Henry!" said

Mum. "You're *NOT* having a packed lunch and that's that."

Horrid Henry and his parents had been fighting about packed lunches for weeks. Henry was desperate to have a packed lunch. Actually, he was desperate *not* to have a school dinner.

Horrid Henry **HATED SCHOOL DINNERS**.

The *stinky* smell. The **TERRIBLE** way Sloppy Sally ladled the food — **splat!** — on his tray so that most

of it **splashed** all over him. And
the food! Queueing for hours for
revolting ravioli and SQUASHED tomatoes.
The LUMPY custard. The **blobby**
mashed potatoes. Horrid Henry could
not bear it any longer.

"Oh please," said Henry. "I'll make
the packed lunch myself." Wouldn't
that be great! He'd fill his lunchbox
with four packs of **crisps**, *chocolate*,
DOUGHNUTS, *cake*, LOLLIES

and one GRAPE. Now that's what I call a
real lunch, thought Henry.

Mum sighed.

Dad sighed.

They looked at each other.

"If you promise that **EVERYTHING** in
your lunchbox will get eaten, then I'll
do a packed lunch for you," said Dad.

"Oh thank you thank you thank you!"
said Horrid Henry. "**EVERYTHING** will
get eaten, I promise." Just not by me,

he thought gleefully. Packed-lunch room, here I come. **Food fights**, *food swaps*, FOOD FUN at last. **Yippee!**

Horrid Henry strolled into the packed-lunch room. He was *KING HENRY THE HORRIBLE*, surveying his unruly subjects. All around him children were **SCREAMING** and **shouting**, *pushing* and shoving, throwing

food and trading treats. Heaven! Horrid
Henry smiled happily and opened his
Terminator Gladiator lunchbox.

Hmmn. An egg salad sandwich. On

brown bread. With crusts. **YUCK!**
But he could always swap it for
one of Greedy Graham's stack of
chocolate spread sandwiches. Or
one of Rude Ralph's *jam rolls*. That
was the great thing about packed
lunches, thought Henry. Someone
always wanted what you had. No one
ever wanted someone else's school
dinner. Henry **shuddered**.

But those **bad days** were behind
him, part of the dim and distant
past. A **horror** story to tell his
grandchildren. Henry could see it

now. A row of **HORRIFIED** toddlers, screaming and crying while he told terrifying tales of stringy stew and **soggy** semolina.

Now, what else? Henry's fingers closed on something round. An apple. Great, thought Henry, he could use it for target practice, and the carrots would be perfect for **poking** Gorgeous Gurinder when she wasn't looking.

Henry dug deeper. What was buried right at the bottom? What was hidden under the *celery sticks* and the granola bar? Oh boy! **Crisps!** Henry loved crisps. So *salty!* So **CRUNCHY!** So yummy! His mean, **horrible** parents only let him have crisps once a week. **Crisps!** What bliss! He could taste their delicious saltiness already. He wouldn't share them with anyone, no matter how hard they begged. Henry tore open the bag and reached in—

Suddenly a **huge shadow** fell over

him. A **FAT** greasy hand shot out.
Snatch! CRUNCH. CRUNCH.

Horrid Henry's crisps
were gone.

Henry was so SHOCKED that
for a moment he could
not speak. "Wha— wha—
what was that?" gasped
Henry as a **GIGANTIC** woman
waddled between the tables. "She just
STOLE my **crisps!**"

"That," said Rude Ralph grimly,
"was Greta. She's the *demon dinner
lady.*"

"Watch out for her!" SQUEALED Sour Susan.

"She's the sneakiest snatcher in school," wailed Weepy William.

What? A dinner lady who SNATCHED food instead of **dumping** it on your plate? How could this be? Henry stared as Greasy Greta patrolled up and down the aisles. Her PIGGY EYES darted from side to side. She ignored Aerobic Al's carrots. She ignored Tidy Ted's yoghurt.

She ignored Goody-Goody Gordon's orange.

Then suddenly—

Snatch! **CHOMP. CHOMP.**

Sour Susan's *sweets* were gone.

Snatch! **CHOMP. CHOMP.**

Dizzy Dave's DOUGHNUT was gone.

Snatch! **CHOMP. CHOMP.**

Beefy Bert's *biscuits* were gone.

Moody Margaret looked up from her lunch.

"Don't look up!" shrieked Susan. Too late! Greasy Greta swept

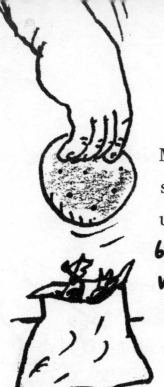

Margaret's food away, stuffing Margaret's uneaten **chocolate bar** into her FAT **wobbly** cheeks.

"HEY, I WASN'T FINISHED!" screamed Margaret.

Greasy Greta ignored her and marched on. Weepy William tried to hide his *toffees* under his cheese sandwich. But Greasy Greta wasn't fooled.

Snatch! **GOBBLE.** **GOBBLE.** The

toffees vanished down Greta's gaping gob.

"WAAAH," wailed William. "I want my toffees!"

"No sweets in school," barked Greasy Greta. She marched UP and DOWN, UP and DOWN, SNATCHING and grabbing, looting and devouring, WOBBLING and gobbling.

Why had no one told him there was a demon dinner lady in charge of the packed-lunch room?

"Why didn't you warn me about her, Ralph?" demanded Henry.

Rude Ralph shrugged. "It wouldn't have done any good. She is unstoppable."

We'll see about that, thought Henry. He *glared* at Greta. No way would Greasy Greta grab his food again.

On Tuesday Greta SNATCHED Henry's DOUGHNUT.

On Wednesday Greta SNATCHED Henry's cake.

On Thursday Greta SNATCHED Henry's *biscuits*.

On Friday, as usual, Horrid Henry persuaded Anxious Andrew to swap his **crisps** for Henry's granola bar. He persuaded Kung-Fu Kate to swap her *chocolates* for Henry's raisins. He persuaded Beefy Bert to swap his **BISCUITS** for Henry's carrots. But what was the use of being a brilliant food trader, thought Henry miserably, if Greasy Greta just *swooped* and snaffled his hard-won treats?

Henry tried hiding his desserts. He tried eating his desserts secretly. He tried tugging them back. But it

was no use. The moment he snapped
open his lunchbox – **SNATCH!**
Greasy Greta grabbed the goodies.

Something had to be done.

"Mum," complained Henry, "there's a **demon dinner lady** at school **SNATCHING** our sweets."

"That's nice, Henry," said Mum, reading her newspaper.

"Dad," complained Henry, "there's a **demon dinner lady** at school **SNATCHING** our sweets."

"Good," said Dad. "You eat too many sweets."

"We're not allowed to bring sweets to school, Henry," said Perfect Peter.

"BUT IT'S NOT FAIR!" squealed Henry. "She takes **crisps**, too."

"If you don't like it, go back to school dinners," said Dad.

"No!" howled Henry. "I **HATE SCHOOL DINNERS!**" WATERY gravy with bits. **Lumpy** surprise with **lumps**. Gristly CLOP with GLOBULES. Food with its own life *slopping* about on his tray. **NO!** Horrid Henry couldn't face it. He'd fought so hard for a packed lunch. Even a packed lunch like the one Dad made, fortified with eight essential minerals and vitamins, was better than going back to **SCHOOL DINNERS**.

He could, of course, just eat healthy foods. Greta never *snatched* those. Henry imagined his lunchbox, groaning with *alfalfa sprouts* on wholemeal brown bread studded with **chewy** bits. **UGH! BLEEEECH! TORTURE!**

He had to keep his packed lunch.
But he had to stop Greta. He just
had to.

And then suddenly Henry had a
brilliant, SPECTACULAR idea. It
was so brilliant that for a moment
he could hardly believe he'd thought
of it. Oh boy, Greta, thought Henry
gleefully, are you going to be sorry
you messed with me.

Lunchtime. Horrid Henry sat with his
lunchbox unopened. Rude Ralph was

armed and ready beside him. Now,
where was Greta?

Thump. Thump. Thump.
The floor shook as the **demon dinner
lady** started her food patrol.

Horrid Henry waited until she was

almost behind him. **SNAP!** He opened his lunchbox.

SNATCH! The familiar greasy hand shot out, *grabbed* Henry's biscuits and *shovelled* them into her mouth. Her **TERRIBLE TEETH** began to chomp.

And then—

"YIAOWWWW! AAAARRRGH!"

A terrible scream echoed through the packed-lunch room.

Greasy Greta turned *purple*. Then *pink*. Then bright *red*.

"YIAOWWWW!" she howled. "I need to cool down! Gimme that!" she screeched, *snatching* Rude Ralph's **DOUGHNUT** and stuffing it in her mouth.

"AAAARRRGH!"

she choked. "I'm on fire! Water! Water!"

She *grabbed* a pitcher of water, poured it on top of herself, then ran howling down the aisle and out the door.

For a moment there was silence. Then the entire packed-lunch room started **clapping** and *cheering*.

"Wow, Henry," said Greedy Graham, "what did you do to her?"

"Nothing," said Horrid Henry. "She just tried my special recipe. Hot chilli powder biscuits, anyone?"

HORRID HENRY

READS A BOOK

Blah blah blah blah blah.

MISS BATTLE-AXE droned on and on and on. **Horrid Henry** drew pictures of *CROCODILES* tucking into a juicy **BATTLE-AXE SNACK** in his maths book.

Snap! Off went her head.

YANK! Bye bye leg.

CRUNCH! Ta-ta teeth.

Yum yum. Henry's crocodile had a big fat smile on its face.

Blah blah blah books **blah blah blah** read **blah blah blah** prize **blah blah blah** . . .

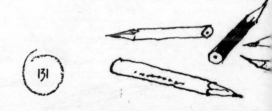

. . . PRIZE?

Horrid Henry stopped doodling.

"WHAT PRIZE?" he shrieked.

"Don't shout out, Henry," said Miss Battle-Axe.

Horrid Henry waved his hand and shouted:

"WHAT PRIZE?"

"Well, Henry, if you'd been paying attention instead of scribbling, you'd know, wouldn't you?" said **MISS BATTLE-AXE**.

Horrid Henry **SCOWLED**. Typical teacher. You're interested enough in

what they're saying to ask a question, and suddenly they don't want to answer.

"So, class, as I was saying before I was so **RUDELY INTERRUPTED**" — she *glared* at Horrid Henry — "you'll have two weeks to read as many books as you can for our school reading competition. Whoever reads the most books will win an **exciting prize**. **A very exciting prize**. But remember, a book report on every book on your list, please."

Oh. A reading competition. Horrid

Henry **slumped** in his chair. PHOOEY. Reading was **HARD, HEAVY WORK**. Just turning the pages made Henry feel **exhausted**. Why couldn't they ever do **FUN** competitions, like whose tummy could *rumble* the loudest, or who **SHOUTED** out the most in class, or who knew the **rudest** words? Horrid Henry would win *those* competitions every time.

But no. **MISS BATTLE-AXE** would never
have a **FUN** competition. Well, no
way was he taking part in a reading
contest. Henry would just have to
watch someone undeserving like
Clever Clare or Brainy Brian swagger
off with the **prize** while he sat
prizeless at the back. **IT WAS SO
UNFAIR!**

"What's the prize?" shouted **MOODY
MARGARET**.

Probably something awful like a
pencil case, thought **Horrid Henry**.
Or a bumper pack of school tea towels.

"Sweets!" shouted Greedy Graham.

"A MILLION POUNDS!" shouted Rude Ralph.

"CLOTHES!" shouted Gorgeous Gurinder.

"A SKATEBOARD!" shouted Aerobic Al.

"A hamster!" said Anxious Andrew.

"Silence!" bellowed MISS BATTLE-AXE. "The prize is a family ticket to a brand new theme park."

Horrid Henry sat up. A THEME PARK! Oh wow! He loved THEME PARKS! Rollercoasters! Water rides! Candy floss! His MEAN, horrible parents never took him to theme parks. They *dragged* him to museums. They **HAULED** him on hikes. But if he **WON** the competition, they'd have to take him. **He had to win that prize.** He had to. But how could he win a **READING** competition without **READING** any books?

"Do COMICS count?" shouted Rude Ralph.

Horrid Henry's heart *leapt*. He was KING OF THE COMIC BOOK READERS. He'd easily win a comic book competition. MISS BATTLE-AXE glared at Ralph with her BEADY eyes.

"OF COURSE NOT!" she said. "Clare! How many books do you think you can read?"

"Fifteen," said Clever Clare.

"Brian?"

"Eighteen," said Brainy Brian.

"Nineteen," said Clare.

"Twenty," said Brian.

Horrid Henry smiled. Wouldn't they get a shock when *he* won the prize? He'd start reading the second he got home.

Horrid Henry **stretched** out in the comfy black chair and switched on the TV. He had plenty of time to read. He'd start tomorrow.

TUESDAY. Oh boy! **FIVE NEW COMICS!** He'd read them first and start on all those books later.

WEDNESDAY. Whoopee! A **Mutant Max** TV special! He'd definitely get reading afterwards.

THURSDAY. Rude Ralph brought round his great new computer game, "**MASH 'EM! SMASH 'EM!**" Henry mashed and smashed and mashed and smashed . . .

FRIDAY. YAWN. Horrid Henry was exhausted after his long, hard week. I'll read **tons** of books tomorrow, thought Henry. After all, there was loads of time till the competition ended.

"How many books have *you* read, Henry?" asked Perfect Peter, looking up from the sofa.

"**LOADS**," lied Henry.

"I've read five," said Perfect Peter proudly. "More than anyone in my class."

"Goody for you," said Henry.

"You're just jealous," said Peter.

"As if I'd ever be jealous of you, **worm**," sneered Henry. He wandered over to the sofa. "So what are you reading?"

"The Happy Nappy," said Peter.

The Happy Nappy! Trust Peter to read a **stupid** book like that.

"What's it about?" asked Henry, snorting.

"It's great," said Peter. "It's all about this nappy—" Then he stopped. "Wait, I'm not telling *you*. You

142

just want to find out so you can use
it in the competition. Well, you're too
late. Tomorrow is the last day."

Horrid Henry felt as if a *dagger*
had been plunged into his heart.
This couldn't be. **Tomorrow!** How had
tomorrow *sneaked* up so fast?

"**WHAT!**" shrieked Henry. "The
competition ends — tomorrow?"

"Yes," said Peter. "You should have
started reading sooner. After all, why
put off till tomorrow what you can do today?"

"**Shut up!**" said Horrid Henry.
He looked around wildly. What to do,

what to do. He had to read something,
anything — fast.

"**GIMME THAT!**" snarled Henry,
SNATCHING Peter's book. Frantically,
he started to read:

"I'm unhappy, pappy," said the
snappy nappy. "A happy nappy is a
clappy—"

Perfect Peter snatched back his book.

"**NO!**" screamed Peter, holding on
tightly. "It's mine."

Henry lunged.

"**Mine!**"

"**MINE!**"

Riii-iippp.

"MUUUUMMMM!" screamed Peter.

"Henry *TORE* my book!"

Mum and Dad ran into the room.

"You're fighting — over a book?" said
Mum. She sat down in a chair.

"I'm speechless," said Mum.

"Well, I'm not," said Dad. "**HENRY! GO
TO YOUR ROOM!**"

"**FINE**!" screamed Horrid Henry.

Horrid Henry *prowled* **UP** and **DOWN** his bedroom. He had to think of something. Fast.

Aha! The room was full of books. He'd just copy down lots of titles. Phew. EASY-PEASY.

And then suddenly Horrid Henry remembered. He had to WRITE a book report for every book he read. *RATS.* **MISS BATTLE-AXE** knew loads and loads of books. She was sure to know the plot of JACK THE KANGAROO or THE ADVENTURES

OF TERRY THE TEA TOWEL.

Well, he'd just have to borrow Peter's list.

Horrid Henry sneaked into Peter's bedroom. There was Peter's competition entry, in the centre of Peter's *immaculate* desk. Henry read it.

Bunny's Big Day
Bounce Goes the Ball
Tickle My Tum
The Happy Nappy
Mouse Goes to Town

Of course Peter would have the **boring** and ~~HORRIBLE~~ Mouse Goes to Town. Could he live with the shame of having baby books like The Happy Nappy and Mouse Goes to Town on his competition entry?

For a day at a THEME PARK, anything.

Quickly, Henry copied Peter's list and book reports. WHOOPEE! Now he had five books. WHEEL OF DEATH here I come, thought Horrid Henry.

Then Henry had to face the **TERRIBLE** truth. Peter's books

wouldn't be enough to win. He'd
heard Clever Clare had seventeen.
If only he didn't have to write those
book reports. Why oh why did
MISS BATTLE-AXE have to know
every book ever written?

And then suddenly Henry had a
brilliant, **SPECTACULAR** idea. It
was so brilliant, and so **simple**, that
Horrid Henry was amazed. Of course
there were books that **MISS BATTLE-AXE**
didn't know. Books that hadn't been
written — yet.

Horrid Henry grabbed his list.

"Mouse Goes to Town. The thrilling adventures of a mouse in town. He meets a dog, a cat and a duck."

Why should that poor mouse just go to town? Quickly Henry began to scribble.

"Mouse Goes to the Country. The thrilling adventures of a mouse in the country. He meets—"

Henry paused. What sort of things *did* you meet in the country? Henry had no idea.

AHA. Henry wrote quickly. "He meets a sheep and a werewolf."

"Mouse Goes Round the World. Mouse discovers that the world is round."

"Mouse Goes to the Loo. The thrilling adventures of one mouse and his potty."

Now, perhaps, something a little different. How about A Boy and his Pig. What could that book be about? thought Henry.

"Once upon a time there was a boy and his pig. They played together every day. The pig went oink."

Sounds good to me, thought Henry.

Then there was A PIG AND HIS BOY. And, of course, A BOYISH PIG. A PIGGISH BOY. TWO PIGS AND A BOY. TWO BOYS AND A PIG.

Horrid Henry wrote and wrote and wrote. When he had filled up four pages with books and reports, and his

hand ached from writing, he stopped and counted.

TWENTY-SEVEN BOOKS! Surely that was more than enough!

MISS BATTLE-AXE rose from her seat and walked to the podium in the school hall. Horrid Henry was so excited he could scarcely breathe. **He had to win**. He was sure to win.

"Well done, everyone," said **MISS BATTLE-AXE**. "So many wonderful books read. But sadly, there can be only one winner."

Me! thought Horrid Henry.

"The winner of the school reading competition, the winner who will be receiving a **fabulous prize**, is" — Horrid Henry got ready to leap up — "Clare, with twenty-eight books!"

Horrid Henry sank back down in his seat as Clever Clare *swaggered* up to the podium. If only he'd added Three Boys, Two Pigs and a Rhinoceros to his list, he'd have tied for first. It was so unfair. All his hard work for nothing.

"Well done, Clare!" beamed **MISS**

BATTLE-AXE. She waved Clare's list.
"I see you've read one of my very
favourites, *Boudicca's Big Battle*."

She stopped. "Oh dear. Clare, you've
put down *Boudicca's Big Battle* twice
by mistake. But never mind. I'm sure
no one else has read twenty-seven
books—"

"I HAVE!"
screamed Horrid
Henry. Leaping
and shouting,
punching the
air with his

fist, **Horrid Henry** ran up on to
the stage, chanting: "**THEME PARK!
THEME PARK! THEME PARK!**"

"**GIMME MY PRIZE!**" he screeched,
SNATCHING the tickets out of Clare's
hand.

"**MINE!**" screamed Clare, **SNATCHING**
them back.

MISS BATTLE-AXE looked grim. She
scanned Henry's list.

"I am not familiar with the Boy and
Pig series," she said.

"That's 'cause it's AUSTRALIAN," said
Horrid Henry.

MISS BATTLE-AXE glared at him. Then she tried to *twist* her face into a smile.

"It appears we have a tie," she said. "Therefore, you will each receive a family pass to the new theme park, **BOOK WORLD**. Congratulations."

Horrid Henry stopped his victory dance.

BOOK WORLD? BOOK WORLD? Surely he'd heard wrong?

"Here are just some of the wonderful attractions you will enjoy at BOOK WORLD," said MISS BATTLE-AXE. "'Thrill to a display of speed-reading! Practise checking out library books! Read to the beat!' Oh my, doesn't that sound FUN!"

"AAAAAARGGGGGGGGG!" screamed Horrid Henry.

HORRID HENRY'S
SCHOOL ELECTION

Yack yack yack yack yack.
Horrid Henry's legs ached. His head ached. His bottom really ached. How much longer would he have to sit on this hard wooden floor and listen to Mrs Oddbod witter on about **hanging** up coats and no *running* in the corridors and walking **down** staircases on the right-hand side? Why were school assemblies so **boring**? If he were head, assemblies would be about the best **TV** programmes, competitions for **gruesome** grub

recipes and speed-eating contests.

Yack yack yack yack yack.

Zoom . . . Zoom . . . Squawk!

Horrid Henry's hawk swooped and
scooped up Mrs Oddbod in his
fearsome beak.

CHOMP.

CHOMP.

CH–

Wait a minute. What was she saying?

"School elections will be held next week," said Mrs Oddbod. "For the first time ever you'll be electing a *School Council President*. Now I want everyone to think of someone they believe would make an outstanding *president*. Someone who will make *important* decisions which will affect everyone, someone worthy of this *high* office, someone who will *represent* this school . . ."

Horrid Henry snorted. School

elections? Phooey! Who'd want to be *School Council President?* All that responsibility . . . all that **power** . . . all that **GLORY** . . . Wait. What was he thinking? Who wouldn't want to be?

Imagine, being *president!* He'd be king, emperor, **LORD HIGH MASTER OF THE UNIVERSE!** He'd make Mrs Oddbod walk the plank. He'd send **MISS BATTLE-AXE** to work in the ship's galley. He'd make playtime last for five hours. He'd ban all salad and vegetables from school dinners and just serve **SWEETS** and

FIZZYWIZZ drinks! And everyone would have to bow down to him as they entered the school! And give him chocolate every day.

President Henry. His Honour, *President Henry.* It had a nice ring. So did King Henry. **EMPEROR HENRY** would be even better though. He'd change his title as soon as he got the throne.

And all he had to do was win the election.

Shout!
Shriek!
"SILENCE!" screeched Mrs Oddbod. "Any more noise and playtime will be cancelled!"

Humph, that was one thing that would never happen when he was *School President*. In fact, he'd make it a rule that anyone who put their hand up in class would get sent to him for punishment. There'd only be shouting out in his school.

"Put up your hand if you wish

166

to nominate someone," said Mrs Oddbod.

Sour Susan's hand shot up.

"I nominate Margaret," she said.

"I accept!" yelled Margaret, preening.

Horrid Henry choked. Margaret? BOSSYBOOTS MARGARET, *President?* She'd be a disaster — a HORRIBLE, *grumpy*, grouchy, *moody* DISASTER. Henry would never hear the end of it. Her head would SWELL so much it would burst. She'd be *swaggering* all over the place,

ordering everyone
around, boasting,
bossing, showing off . . .

Horrid Henry's hand shot up.

"I nominate . . . **ME!**" he shrieked.

"You?" said Mrs Oddbod coldly.

"Me," said **Horrid Henry**.

"I second it," shouted Rude Ralph.

Henry beamed at Ralph. He'd make
Ralph his
Grand Vizier.
Or maybe
LORD HIGH
EXECUTIONER.

"Any more nominations?" said Mrs Oddbod. She looked unhappy. "Come on, Bert, what would you do to improve the school?"

"I dunno," said Bert.

"Clare?" said Mrs Oddbod.

"More fractions!" said Clare.

Horrid Henry caught Ralph's eye.

"*Boo!*" yelled Ralph. "Down with Clare!"

"Yeah, boo!" yelled Dizzy Dave.

"**Boo!**" hissed Horrid Henry.

"Last chance to nominate anyone else," said Mrs Oddbod desperately.

Silence.

"All right," said Mrs Oddbod, "you have two candidates for President. Posters can be displayed from tomorrow. Speeches the day after tomorrow. Good luck to both candidates."

Horrid Henry glared at MOODY MARGARET.

MOODY MARGARET glared at **Horrid Henry**.

I'll beat that **GRUMPFACE** frog if it's the last thing I do, thought Horrid Henry.

I'll beat that pongy pants pimple if it's the last thing I do, thought **MOODY MARGARET**.

"Vote Margaret! Margaret for *President!*" trilled Sour Susan the next day, as she and Margaret handed out leaflets during playtime.

"**HA HA**, Henry, I'm going to win, and you're not!" chanted Margaret, sticking out her tongue.

"Yeah, Henry, Margaret's going to win," said Sour Susan.

"Oh yeah?" said Henry. Wait till she saw his fantastic campaign posters with the big picture of KING HENRY THE HORRIBLE.

"Yeah."

"We'll see about that," said Horrid Henry.

He'd better start campaigning at once. Now, whose votes could he count on?

Ralph's for sure. And, **uh** . . . **um** . . . **uhMMMM** . . . Ralph.

Toby might vote for him but he'd probably have to beg. **HMMM**. Two votes were not enough to win. He'd have to get more support. Well, no time like the present to remind everyone what a **great guy** he was.

Zippy Zoe zipped past. **Horrid Henry** smiled at her. Zoe stopped dead.

"Why are you smiling at me, Henry?" said Zippy Zoe. She checked to see

if she'd come to school wearing
pyjamas or if her jumper had a
BIG HOLE.

"Just because it's so nice to see
you," said Horrid Henry. "Will you
vote for me for *president?*"

Zoe stared at him.

"Margaret gave me
a pencil with her
name on it," said
Zoe. "And a
sticker. What
will you give
me?"

Give? Give? **Horrid Henry** liked getting. He did not like giving. So Margaret was bribing people, was she? Well, two could play at that game. He'd bring loads of **SWEETS** into school tomorrow and hand them out to everyone who promised to vote for him. That would guarantee victory!

And he'd make sure that everyone had to give him sweets after he'd won.

Anxious Andrew walked by wearing a "Margaret for *President*" sticker.

"Oooh, Andrew, I wouldn't vote for her," said Henry. "Do you know what she's planning to do?" Henry whispered in Andrew's ear. Andrew GASPED.

"No," said Andrew.

"Yes," said Henry. "And ban crisps, too. You know what an old BOSSYBOOTS Margaret is."

Henry handed him a leaflet.

Andrew looked uncertain.

"Vote for me and I'll make you *Vice-Chairman of the Presidential Snacks Sub-Committee.*"

"Oooh," said Andrew.

Henry promised the same job to Dizzy Dave, Jolly Josh and Weepy William.

He promised Needy Neil his mum could sit with him in class. He promised Singing Soraya she could sing every day in assembly. He promised Greedy Graham there'd be ice cream every day for lunch.

The election is in the bag, thought **Horrid Henry** gleefully. He fingered the magic marker in his pocket. **TEE HEE**. Just wait till Margaret saw how he was planning to **GRAFFITI** her poster! And wasn't it lucky it was impossible to graffiti his name or change it to something rude. Shame, thought **Horrid Henry**, that Peter wasn't running for *president*. If you crossed out the "t" and the "r" you'd get "Vote for Pee".

Horrid Henry *strolled* over to the wall where the campaign posters were displayed.

Huh?
what?

A **TERRIBLE** sight met his eyes. His "Vote for Henry" posters had been defaced. Instead of his crowned head,

a **HORRIBLE** picture of a **chicken's head** had been glued on top of his body. And the 'ry' of his name had been crossed out.

Beneath it was written:

CLUCK CLUCK YUCK! VOTE FOR A HEN? NO WAY!

What a dirty trick, thought **Horrid Henry** indignantly. How dare Margaret deface his posters! Just because he'd handed out leaflets showing Margaret with a 𝔽ℝ𝕆𝔾'𝕊 face. Margaret was a frog-face. The school needed to know the truth about her.

Well, no more *Mr Nice Guy*. This was **WAR**.

MOODY MARGARET entered the playground. A *TERRIBLE* sight met her eyes. All her "Vote Margaret" posters had been defaced. **Huge** beards and moustaches had been drawn on every one. Beneath the picture, instead of "Be on target! Vote Margaret!" the words now read:

The next poster read:

How dare Henry **GRAFFITI** over her posters! I'll get you, Henry, thought Margaret. Just wait until tomorrow.

The next day was campaign speech day. **Horrid Henry** sat on the stage with **MOODY MARGARET** in front of the entire school. He was armed and ready. Margaret would be blasted from the race. As Margaret rose to speak, Henry made a *HORRIBLE* **gagging** face.

"We face a great danger," said **MOODY MARGARET**. "Do you want a *leader* like me? Or a **LOSER** like Henry? Do you want someone who will make you **PROUD** of this school?

Or someone like Henry who will make you ASHAMED? I will be the best *president* ever. I'm already **CAPTAIN OF THE FOOTBALL TEAM**. I know how to tell people what to do. This school will be heaven with me in charge. Remember, a vote for me will brighten every school day."

"Go, Margaret!" yelled Sour Susan as Margaret sat down.

Horrid Henry rose to speak.

"When I'm *president*," said Horrid Henry, "I promise a **Goo-Shooter** day! I promise a **GROSS-OUT** day! With

my best friend **Marvin the Maniac** presenting the prize. School will start at lunchtime, and end after playtime. **GOBBLE AND GO** will run the school cafeteria. I promise no homework! I promise **SKATEBOARDING** in the hall! I promise **ice cream!** And **SWEETS!**

"If you vote for **MARGARET**, you'll get a **dictator**. And how do I know this? Because I have discovered her **TOP-SECRET** plans!" **Horrid Henry** pulled out a piece of paper covered in writing and showed it to the hall.

185

Margaret's Top Secret Plans for when I am President

The school day is too short. School will end at 6.00 when I'm in charge

I look at my school lunch and I think, 'Why is there a dessert on my plate when there should be more vegetables?' All sweets and desserts will be banned

"Just listen to what she wrote."

There isn't enough homework at this school. Five hours of homework every night

Get rid of school holidays. Who needs them?

Ban chips!

Ban football!

Ban playtime!

"**I NEVER WROTE THAT!**" screeched Margaret.

"She would say that, wouldn't she?" said Henry *smoothly*. "But the voters need to know the truth."

"He's lying!" shouted Margaret.

"Don't be fooled, everyone! Margaret will ban **SWEETS!** Margaret will ban *crisps!* Margaret will make you do lots more homework. Margaret wants to have school **seven days a week**.

"So vote **Henry** if you want to stop this *evil fiend!* Vote **Henry** for loads of **SWEETS!** Vote **Henry** for loads of

FUN! Vote **Henry** for *president!*"

"HENRY! HENRY! HENRY!"

shouted Ralph, as Henry sat down
to rapturous applause.

He'd done it! He'd won! And by a
landslide. Yes! He was *President
Lord High Master of the Universe!*
Just wait till he started **bossing**
everyone around! Margaret had been
defeated — at last!

Mrs Oddbod *glared* at Henry as they sat in her office after the results had been announced. She looked grey.

"As *president*, you will call the school council meeting to order. You will organise the **toilet tidy rota**. You will lead the LITTER COLLECTION every playtime."

Horrid Henry's knees felt weak. *Toilet . . . tidy . . . rota?* LITTER?

What?? That was his job?

That's why he'd schemed and bribed and fought and campaigned and given away all those SWEETS?

Where was his throne? His title? His power?

NOOO!

"I resign!" said Horrid Henry.

HORRID HENRY
TERRIBLE TEACHERS

Turn the
page for lots of
fun games and
activities!

wordsearch

CAN YOU FIND ALL THE SCHOOL-RELATED WORDS
IN THE GRID BELOW?

D	L	Y	F	B	R	D	K	E	B	O	S
I	H	O	M	E	W	O	R	K	O	V	F
N	F	B	Y	R	A	K	U	E	O	S	M
N	E	D	D	I	N	G	O	F	K	C	C
E	V	N	R	F	I	P	Y	H	S	H	L
R	T	T	G	O	C	A	I	S	E	P	A
L	E	S	S	O	N	E	J	M	R	Q	S
A	A	C	R	T	P	E	N	C	I	L	S
D	C	H	T	B	A	F	I	M	T	A	R
Y	H	R	U	A	N	E	D	N	C	H	O
S	E	F	P	L	I	B	R	A	R	Y	O
B	R	T	S	L	X	Q	P	V	Z	L	M

PENCILS   TEACHER   LESSON
LIBRARY   BOOKS   HOMEWORK
DINNER LADY   FOOTBALL   CLASSROOM

Maze

CAN YOU HELP HENRY FIND HIS WAY THROUGH THE
MAZE TO ESCAPE THE DEMON DINNER LADY?

Would You Rather?

HENRY WOULD RATHER WATCH TELEVISION THAN READ A BOOK. HERE ARE SOME REALLY TRICKY CHOICES TO OFFER YOUR FRIENDS!

1. Would you rather be able to read your teacher's mind or be invisible?

2. Would you rather eat ice cream for every meal or never again?

3. Would you rather be a film star or a football champion?

4. Would you rather never have to go to school or never have to do any chores?

5. Would you rather have a sleepover in a jungle or in a desert?

6. Would you rather squawk like a chicken or waddle like a duck?

Would You Rather?

7. Would you rather find a pot of gold or a unicorn?

8. Would you rather have really good hearing or a super sense of smell?

9. Would you rather meet a snake or a tarantula?

10. Would you rather live in a cave or a treehouse?

Spot the Difference

CAN YOU FIND FIVE DIFFERENCES
BETWEEN THE PICTURES?

Jolly Jokes

HENRY AND HIS FRIENDS LOVE TELLING JOKES. WHY NOT TRY SOME OF THESE ON YOUR FRIENDS?

What's a witch's favourite subject at school?

SPELLING!

Why did the dog do so well at school?

BECAUSE HE WAS THE TEACHER'S PET.

How do you get straight As at school?

USE A RULER!

Which dinosaur knew the most words?

THE THESAURUS.

Why did the music teacher need a ladder?

TO REACH THE HIGH NOTES.

Why did the teacher wear sunglasses to school?

BECAUSE HER CLASS WERE SO BRIGHT!

What do snakes learn at school?

HISS-TORY.

Why did the child eat his homework?

BECAUSE THE TEACHER SAID IT WAS A PIECE OF CAKE!

Why is 2 + 2 = 5 like your left foot?

IT'S NOT RIGHT.

Why did the teacher write on the window?

TO MAKE THE LESSON VERY CLEAR!

cool school crossword

CAN YOU WORK OUT THE MISSING WORDS AND FIT THEM INTO THE GRID?

ACROSS

1. HENRY HATES WRITING BOOK _ _ _ _ _ _ _ (7)

2. HENRY WANTS TO CHANGE FROM SCHOOL DINNERS TO _ _ _ _ _ _ LUNCH (6)

3. PETER IS PRACTISING HIS _ _ _ _ _ _ _ _ DANCE (8)

4. THE EGG AND _ _ _ _ _ RACE WAS A DISASTER! (5)

DOWN

5. MOODY MARGARET IS ALSO STANDING IN THE SCHOOL _ _ _ _ _ _ _ _ (8)

6. MISBEHAVING ON A SCHOOL TRIP MEANS YOU'LL BE SENT TO THE _ _ _ (CHILDREN'S ROOM) (3)

7. THE _ _ _ _ _ DINNER LADY IS TRULY TERRIFYING (5)

Spot the Difference

CAN YOU FIND FIVE DIFFERENCES BETWEEN THE PICTURES?

clever clare's Riddles

DO YOU KNOW THE ANSWERS TO THESE BRAINTEASERS?
TRY THEM ON YOUR FRIENDS AND FAMILY!

I can fill a room, but take up no
space. What am I?
Light.

What can you catch, but not throw?
A cold.

What gets wetter the more it dries?
A towel.

I am an odd number, but if you take away
a letter I am even. What am I?
Seven.